Kart Master

HESSLE MOUNT SCHOOL

Phil Kettle
illustrated by Craig Smith

SCHOLASTIC
SYDNEY AUCKLAND NEW YORK TORONTO LONDON
MEXICO CITY NEW DELHI HONG KONG

LEXILE™ 480

Scholastic Education
345 Pacific Highway
Lindfield NSW 2070
an imprint of Scholastic Australia Pty Limited (ABN 11 000 614 577)
PO Box 579, Gosford NSW 2250.
www.scholastic.com.au
www.toocoolrules.com

Part of the Scholastic Group
Sydney ● Auckland ● New York ● Toronto ● London ● Mexico City
● New Delhi ● Hong Kong

First published by Scholastic Education in 2001.
Text copyright © Phillip Kettle, 2001.
Illustrations copyright © black dog books and Springhill Pty Ltd, 2001.

🐕 a black dog and Springhill book

National Library of Australia Cataloguing-in-Publication entry
Kettle, Phillip, 1955-
    Toocool, Kart Master.
    ISBN 1 86504 339 7.
    1. Karting - Juvenile fiction. I. Smith, Craig, 1955-.
    II. Title. (Series: Toocool).
A823.4

Typeset in Plantin.
Printed by McPherson's Printing Group, Maryborough Vic.

10 9 8 7 6 5 4 3 2   1 2 3 4 5 / 0

Contents

Toocool

Marcy

Noel

Spike

Dog

Simon

Eddie

Chapter 1

Signing Up

Spike and I were walking through the park, talking about our last game of cricket. Marcy came zooming up on her bike.

"Get out of my way, Toocool, or I'll squash you like a lemon."

We leaped off the bike track and into the bushes. Marcy raced past us.

"Toocool, have a look at the noticeboard," she yelled.

Spike and I walked over to the noticeboard. It said:

Entrants Wanted
TC Park, Kart Race.

Spike scribbled his name on the list. Marcy's name was already there. Simon, who was in a wheelchair, said he was the fastest thing on wheels. He said he would win easily.

Noel, who always chewed his sleeve, was also going to enter.

Even Eddie stopped eating long enough to write his name on the list.

I told them all to give up
while they could—I was going
to be a famous racing car
driver. I told them this kart
race was only the beginning of
my amazing racing career.

Eddie laughed. "You better stay out of my way, Toocool, or you'll be eating my dust."

"You won't get past the starting line, Eddie," I said.

Eddie went to throw his cake at me. But he changed his mind. He decided it was too good to waste.

I had one week to build the greatest racing kart the world had ever seen.

"Come on, Dog," I said. "We're going home to build the world's greatest racing kart."

"The second greatest," said Spike. "Mine will be best."

"Mine's nearly finished," said Marcy, as she rode away. "You two have no hope."

Chapter 2

The Coolest Kart

Everyone hurried home.
I ran straight out to the
workshop. I was thinking
about Marcy. Her kart was
nearly finished. She would have
lots of time to test drive it.
I would have to get moving if
mine was going to beat hers.

Once I was in the workshop
I felt better. I had already built
spaceships in there, so building
a kart would be easy.

It wasn't long before I had heaps of stuff all over the floor. I was working at top speed— until a voice came over the fence.

"What's all that noise? Can't you do anything that's not noisy?"

It was old Tom from the house next door.

9

"I'm building a kart for the big race on Saturday," I told him. "I'm going to win."

"Toocool, when I was your age I built the fastest karts on this block."

"Why don't you help me build my kart, sir?" I said.

"Just keep the noise down," he grumbled.

The kart was taking shape. I covered a cardboard box with tin foil. It looked like a real motor. And Dog's lead made a great steering cord.

Next I strapped an old pillow to the seat for extra comfort. Then I used its pillowcase to make the Toocool flag. I hung the flag from a stick taped to the back.

The kart looked really cool. All it needed was wheels.

I decided I could do without my old bike. That gave me two wheels. And I hadn't seen Mum use her golf buggy for a while. That gave me two more wheels.

Gee, this was a great kart. Anyone who thought they could beat me was dreaming. Even Marcy.

The last thing I had to do was paint the kart. Dad had some red paint. He bought it to paint the roof. I decided that red was the best colour for a champion's kart. I slapped on a few coats.

I had a few spills with the paint. But I knew Dad would understand. I was under a lot of pressure.

Chapter 3
A Tense Week

One week to go and the tension was high in TC Park.

Noel chewed two new holes in his sleeve.

Eddie went home crying after Marcy told him he couldn't eat cakes on the kart.

Simon didn't say much to anyone. But his new T-shirt said, *Fastest Kid On Wheels*.

Spike and I spent our time walking around the racetrack. I pointed out to Spike where I would pass him. I told him why I was going to win. Spike took it well.

I went to bed on Friday
night dreaming of the big race.
Dreaming of my victory.
Dreaming of the trophy I was
going to win. Dreaming of my
shiny red kart.

Chapter 4
A Close Race

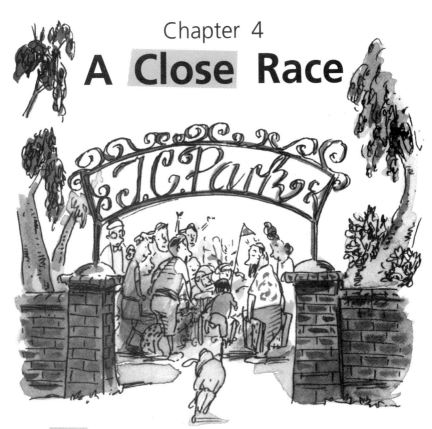

On Saturday morning there was a huge crowd at TC park. They had come to check out the karts. But mostly they had come to see Toocool, the Kart Master, drive like a legend.

I led my kart to
the starting line.
I knew it was the coolest kart
there. But Marcy said it was a
piece of junk.

"Toocool, your kart is a
piece of junk."

"Drivers, start your engines," yelled Eddie's dad. The sound was deafening as we revved our engines.

I wondered what old Tom thought of noise like this! I looked over at him. He was busy reading the newspaper.

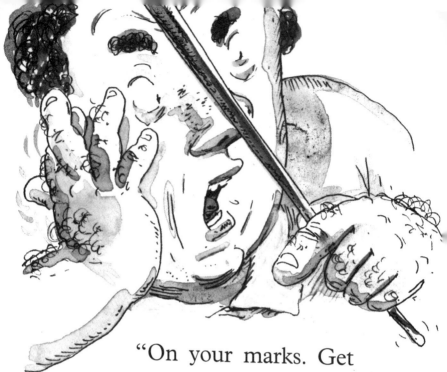

"On your marks. Get set. Go!" yelled Eddie's dad.

Simon broke away first. He was in front—until Dog chased a pigeon across the track. Simon swerved and his chair hit the gutter. It bounced into the air, landed on its wheels and kept going. But it slowed Simon right down.

Noel kept to the edge of the track. He was rolling along okay. It was the first time I'd seen Noel without his sleeve in his mouth.

The Toocool machine was really firing. I stared ahead. The first speed hump was coming up. It wouldn't be long before I made my winning move.

Eddie hit the speed hump
first. His kart flew through the
air like a bird, but it landed like
a brick. The four wheels went
in different directions. Eddie
was left sitting in the middle of
the track. I had to swerve
around him.

While that was going on, Marcy made her move. "Out of my way or I'll squash you all...like lemons!" she yelled. Simon didn't listen and he nosed in front of her. Spike stayed right beside me. Noel sat just behind us.

It was a close race. There was only 100 metres to go. And one more speed hump to get over.

Chapter 5
Flying Karts

We all hit the speed hump at the same time.

My kart went flying. I hit Simon in mid-air. Simon hit Marcy. Marcy hit Spike. Noel hit the gutter.

That was the last thing I saw before I shut my eyes.

When I opened my eyes,
there were people everywhere.
It was like a disaster movie.

Mum was kneeling over me.
"Toocool, are you all right?"

"Did I win?" I asked.

Then I heard Eddie's dad.
He said the race was cancelled.
Oh no! He said there wouldn't
be another race until next year.

I walked home, dragging my mangled kart behind me. Being a champion wasn't always easy. I would have won if the others hadn't been such terrible drivers.

Old Tom stuck his head over the fence. He said he could have beaten me.

"Toocool, if I had been in that race, you would have been eating my dust."

Old Tom is such a dreamer.

I shoved the kart into the corner of Dad's shed. It made a loud scraping noise as it rubbed up against Dad's old tin boat. That gave me an idea.

Tomorrow I would give Bloggsy a call.

It was time to go fishing.

The End!

Toocool's
Kart Glossary

Pit crew—A group of people who help you during the race. The pit crew have to work fast so you can get back in the race.

Revved—The drivers revved their engines. This means they turned up their engines to get ready to go fast.

Sponsors—People who pay you to wear their clothes or their logo. If you are a big star, you get more sponsors.

Swerve—To turn suddenly.

Victory—If you have a victory it means you have won.

Toocool's Map
of TC Park

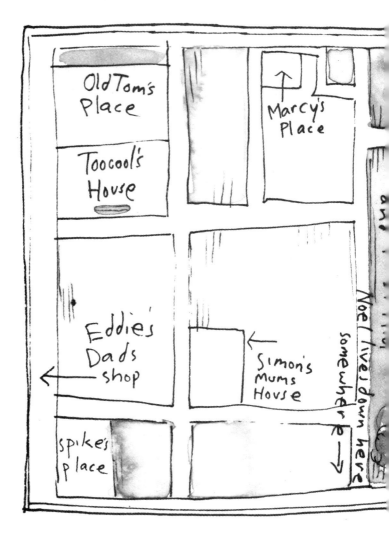

Old Tom's
Place

Toocool's
House

Marcy's
Place

Eddie's
Dad's
shop

Simon's
Mums
House

Noel lives down here somewhere

spike's
place

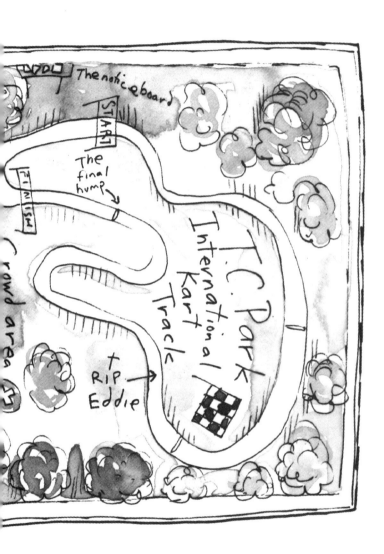

Toocool's Quick Summary
of kart racing

Kart racing started in America in 1957. Soon people in many other countries joined in. Different countries have different rules, but the karts are nearly always small and simple.

Karts are often called "go-karts." I think it's because their drivers are always yelling, "Go kart, go!"

Karts have four wheels and they only sit one person. Karts are also very close to the ground and most of them don't have a roof. Some of them can go over 200 kilometres per hour!

Kart drivers wear the same clothes as racing car drivers. They wear a helmet and goggles and a full bodysuit. They look really cool.

Many racing car drivers start out driving karts.

The **Kart**

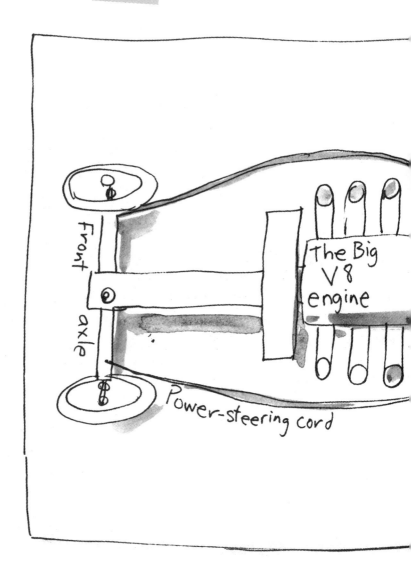

Front

axle

The Big
V8
engine

Power-steering cord

34

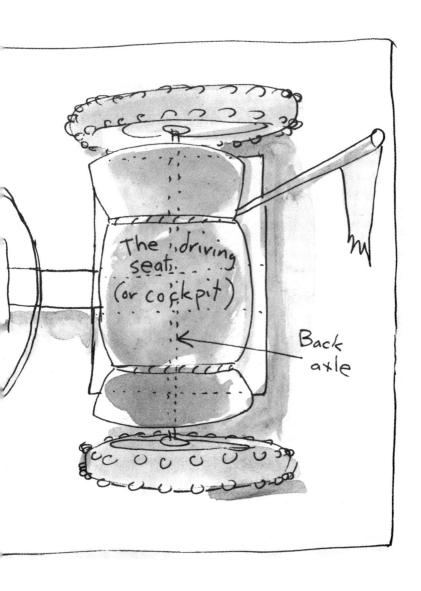

The driving seat
(or cockpit)

Back axle

35

Q & A with Toocool—
he answers his own questions

 **How long have you been interested in karts?**

I've always loved karts. It started when I was a baby. I remember sitting in my pram and thinking what a great kart it would make.

What are the best kind of wheels for a kart?

The best wheels are the ones that don't cost anything. Wheels from an old pram are good. Some old lawn mowers have great wheels. But don't take wheels from your sister's bike. She won't be happy.

Should you take passengers in your kart?

I think it would be a great idea. But every time I ask someone to come for a ride they say no. Even when I ask Dog, he runs away. So maybe it's not a good idea.

Do karts have a radio?

No way! You wouldn't be able to hear it. Kart motors are very loud.

Do you always wear a helmet on your kart?

Yes. I've got a special helmet for the kart. It's got stickers. I have many sponsors. They like to see a champion wear their stickers.

Have you and your kart ever been on television?

Yes. Most of the races I have been in have been on TV. But I never get to see it because I'm racing. Motor racing is always shown live from the racetrack.

When do you think you will be in Formula One racing?

It won't be long. I just have to grow a bit more. I can almost reach the pedals in a racing car.

And I can easily see over the steering wheel. I will probably be the youngest racing car driver ever.

Who will be in your pit crew?

Most of my friends want to be in my pit crew. They always say, "Toocool, we want to be in your pit crew." I'm not sure how many people are allowed in a pit crew. I think the best drivers have the biggest pit crews.

Kart Quiz
How much do you know about kart racing?

Q1 What side of the track should you race on?
A. The left side. **B.** The right side. **C.** Either side.

Q2 Do kart drivers wear seat belts?
A. Always. **B.** When they remember. **C.** No.

Q3 How much petrol does a kart like Toocool's use?
A. Heaps. **B.** None. **C.** A tiny bit.

Q4 What colour are the fastest karts?

A. Red. *B.* White. *C.* Brown.

Q5 What does a pit crew do?

A. Repairs and re-fuelling.

B. Yell at the driver.

C. Tow the kart away.

Q6 When do kart drivers wear a helmet?

A. Whenever they are in the kart.

B. When they forget their sunscreen.

C. When it's cold.

Q7 If you took two wheels off your kart, what would it do?

A. Stop. *B.* Crash. *C.* Go faster.

Q8 If you saw Toocool in his kart, what would you do?

A. Give him a cheer. **B.** Ask for a ride. **C.** Find somewhere to hide.

Q9 Which is the fastest?
A. Racing car. **B.** Racehorse.
C. Toocool's kart.

Q10 Who will be the next world champion racing car driver?
A. Marcy. **B.** Eddie. **C.** Toocool.

ANSWERS

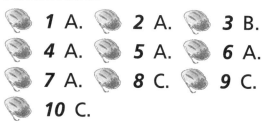

1 A.   *2* A.   *3* B.
4 A.   *5* A.   *6* A.
7 A.   *8* C.   *9* C.
10 C.

If you got ten questions right, you are almost ready to race. If you got more than five right, stay on your bike a bit longer. If you got less than five right, you should keep walking.

TOOCOOL

Fishing Fanatic

At sunrise **Toocool** will grapple with the giant of the deep—the marlin he dreams of catching. Has **Toocool** met his match? Let the battle begin.

Other titles in the **Toocool** series:

Toocool Tennis Ace
Toocool Footy Hero
Toocool Slam Dunk Magician
Toocool Grand Prix Champ
Toocool Cricket Legend
Toocool Surfing Pro